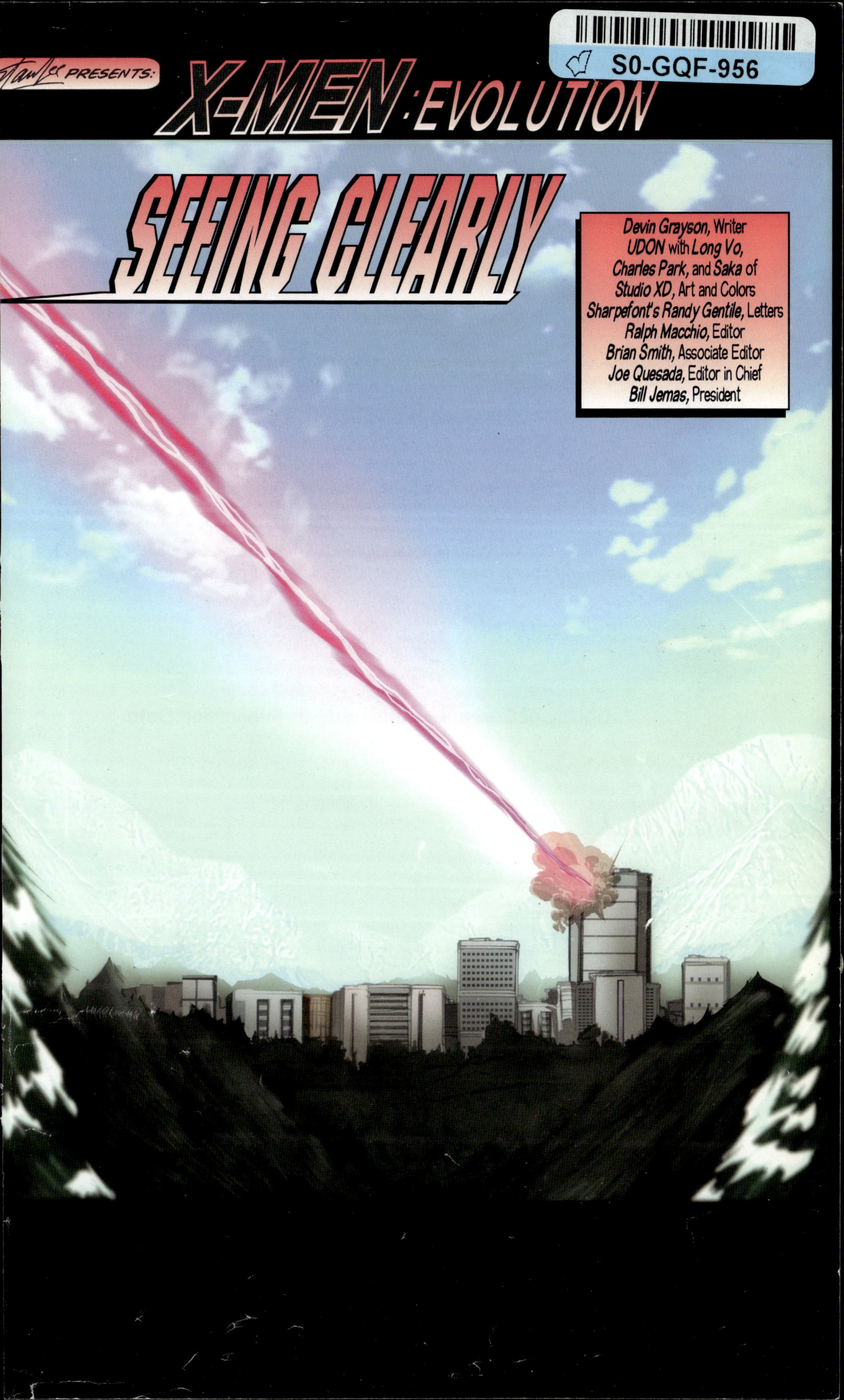
Stan Lee PRESENTS:
X-MEN : EVOLUTION
SEEING CLEARLY
Devin Grayson, Writer
UDON with Long Vo,
Charles Park, and Saka of
Studio XD, Art and Colors
Sharpefont's Randy Gentile, Letters
Ralph Macchio, Editor
Brian Smith, Associate Editor
Joe Quesada, Editor in Chief
Bill Jemas, President

VISIT US AT
www.abdopub.com

Spotlight, a division of ABDO Publishing Company Inc., is the school and library distributor of the Marvel Entertainment books.

Library bound edition © 2006

MARVEL, and all related character names and the distinctive likenesses thereof are trademarks of Marvel Characters, Inc., and is/are used with permission. Copyright © 2005 Marvel Characters, Inc. All rights reserved. www.marvel.com

MARVEL, X-Men: TM & © 2005 Marvel Characters, Inc. All rights reserved. www.marvel.com. This book is produced under license from Marvel Characters, Inc.

Library of Congress Cataloging-in-Publication Data

Seeing Clearly

ISBN 1-59961-055-8   (Reinforced Library Bound Edition)

All Spotlight books are reinforced library binding and manufactured in the United States of America

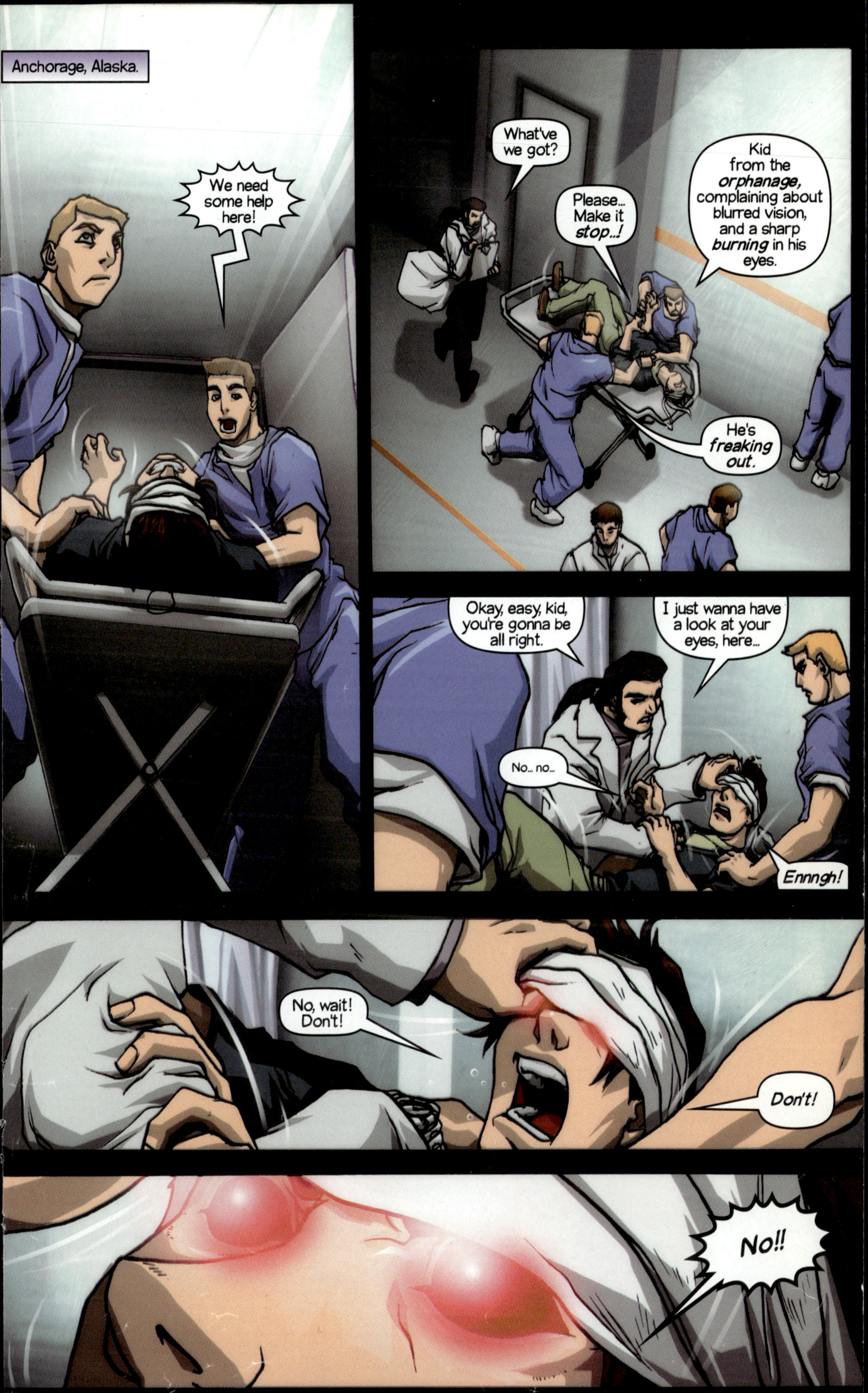
Anchorage, Alaska.
We need some help here!
What've we got?
Please... Make it *stop*...!
Kid from the *orphanage,* complaining about blurred vision, and a sharp *burning* in his eyes.
He's *freaking out.*
Okay, easy, kid, you're gonna be all right.
I just wanna have a look at your eyes, here...
No... no...
Ennngh!
No, wait! Don't!
Don't!
No!!

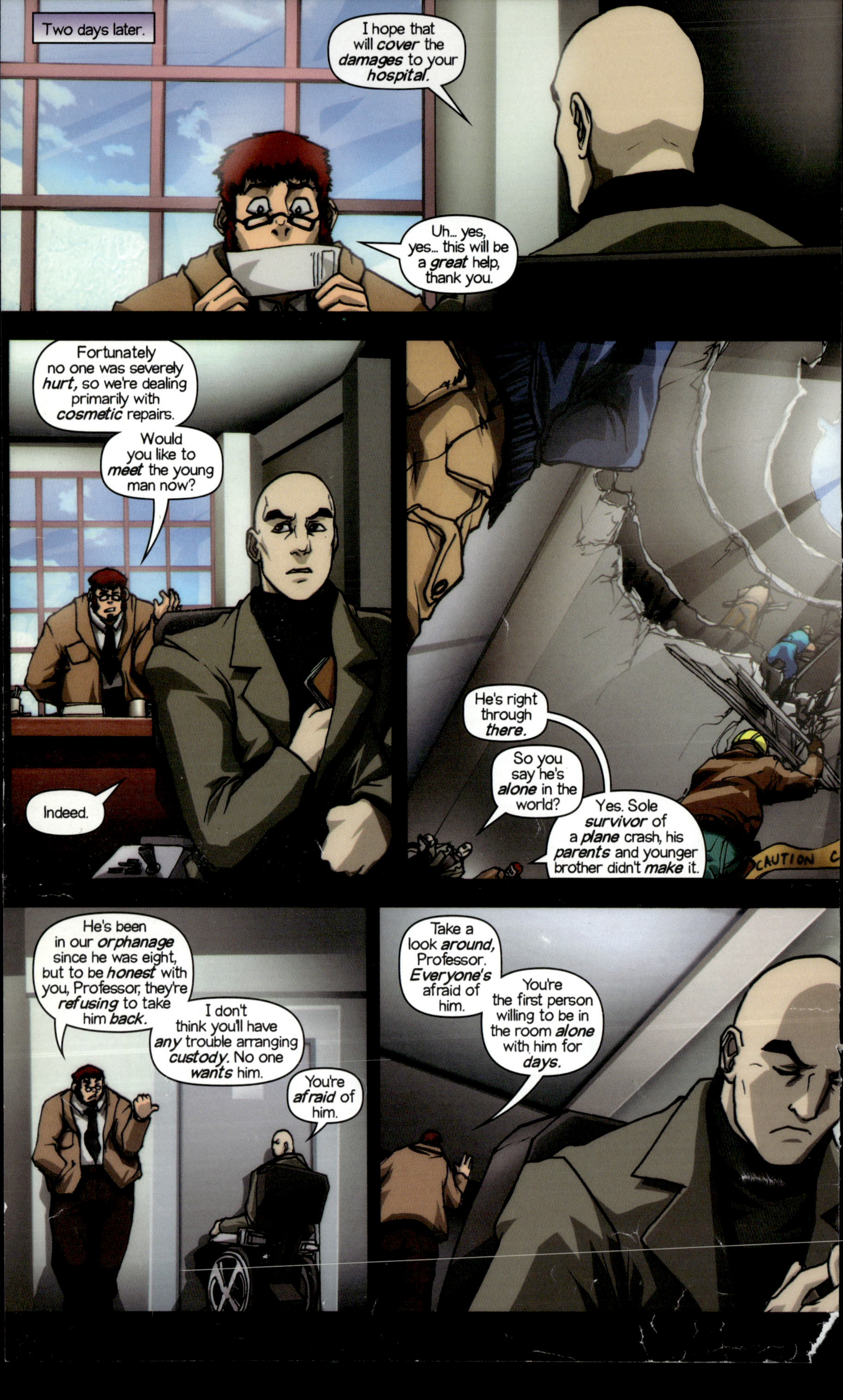
Two days later.
I hope that will *cover* the *damages* to your *hospital.*
Uh... yes, yes... this will be a *great* help, thank you.
Fortunately no one was severely *hurt,* so we're dealing primarily with *cosmetic* repairs.
Would you like to *meet* the young man now?
Indeed.
He's right through *there.*
So you say he's *alone* in the world?
Yes. Sole *survivor* of a *plane* crash, his *parents* and younger brother didn't *make* it.
CAUTION
He's been in our *orphanage* since he was eight, but to be *honest* with you, Professor, they're *refusing* to take him *back.*
I don't think you'll have *any* trouble arranging *custody.* No one *wants* him.
You're *afraid* of him.
Take a look *around,* Professor. *Everyone's* afraid of him.
You're the first person willing to be in the room *alone* with him for *days.*

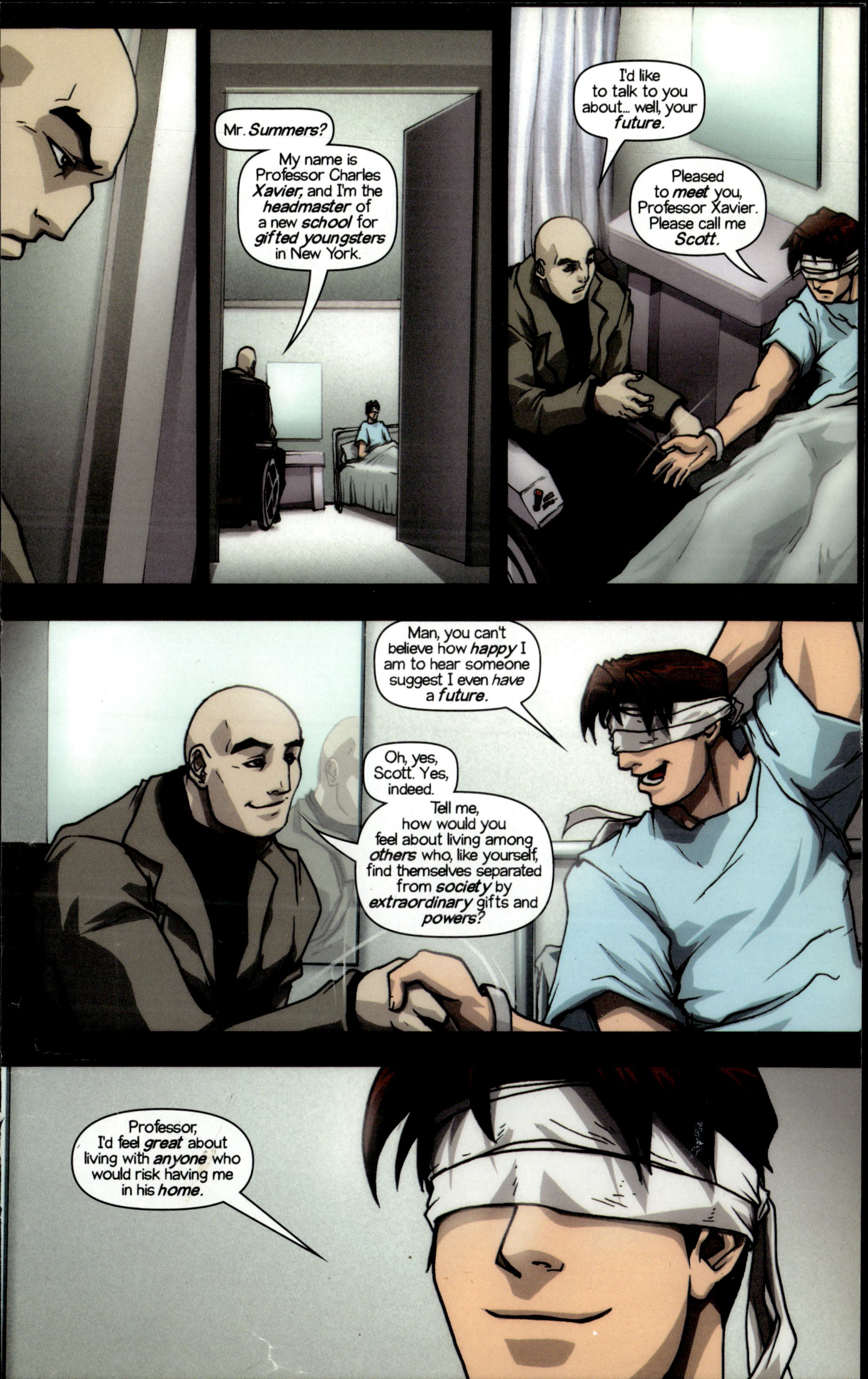
Mr. Summers?
My name is Professor Charles Xavier, and I'm the headmaster of a new school for gifted youngsters in New York.
I'd like to talk to you about... well, your future.
Pleased to meet you, Professor Xavier. Please call me Scott.
Man, you can't believe how happy I am to hear someone suggest I even have a future.
Oh, yes, Scott. Yes, indeed.
Tell me, how would you feel about living among others who, like yourself, find themselves separated from society by extraordinary gifts and powers?
Professor, I'd feel great about living with anyone who would risk having me in his home.

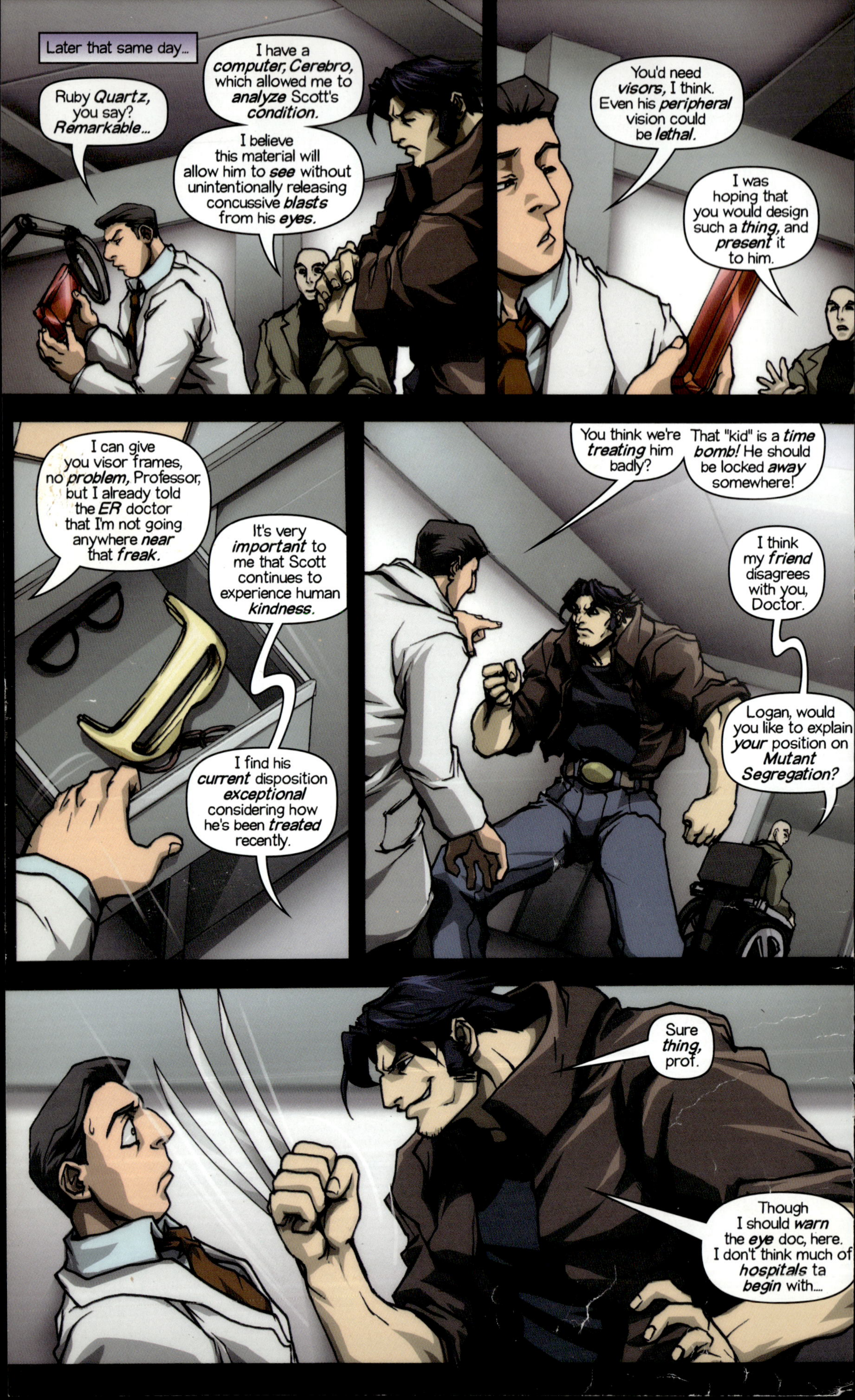

Later that same day...
Ruby Quartz, you say? Remarkable...
I have a computer, Cerebro, which allowed me to analyze Scott's condition.
I believe this material will allow him to see without unintentionally releasing concussive blasts from his eyes.
You'd need visors, I think. Even his peripheral vision could be lethal.
I was hoping that you would design such a thing, and present it to him.
I can give you visor frames, no problem, Professor, but I already told the ER doctor that I'm not going anywhere near that freak.
It's very important to me that Scott continues to experience human kindness.
I find his current disposition exceptional considering how he's been treated recently.
You think we're treating him badly?
That "kid" is a time bomb! He should be locked away somewhere!
I think my friend disagrees with you, Doctor.
Logan, would you like to explain your position on Mutant Segregation?
Sure thing, prof.
Though I should warn the eye doc, here. I don't think much of hospitals ta begin with....

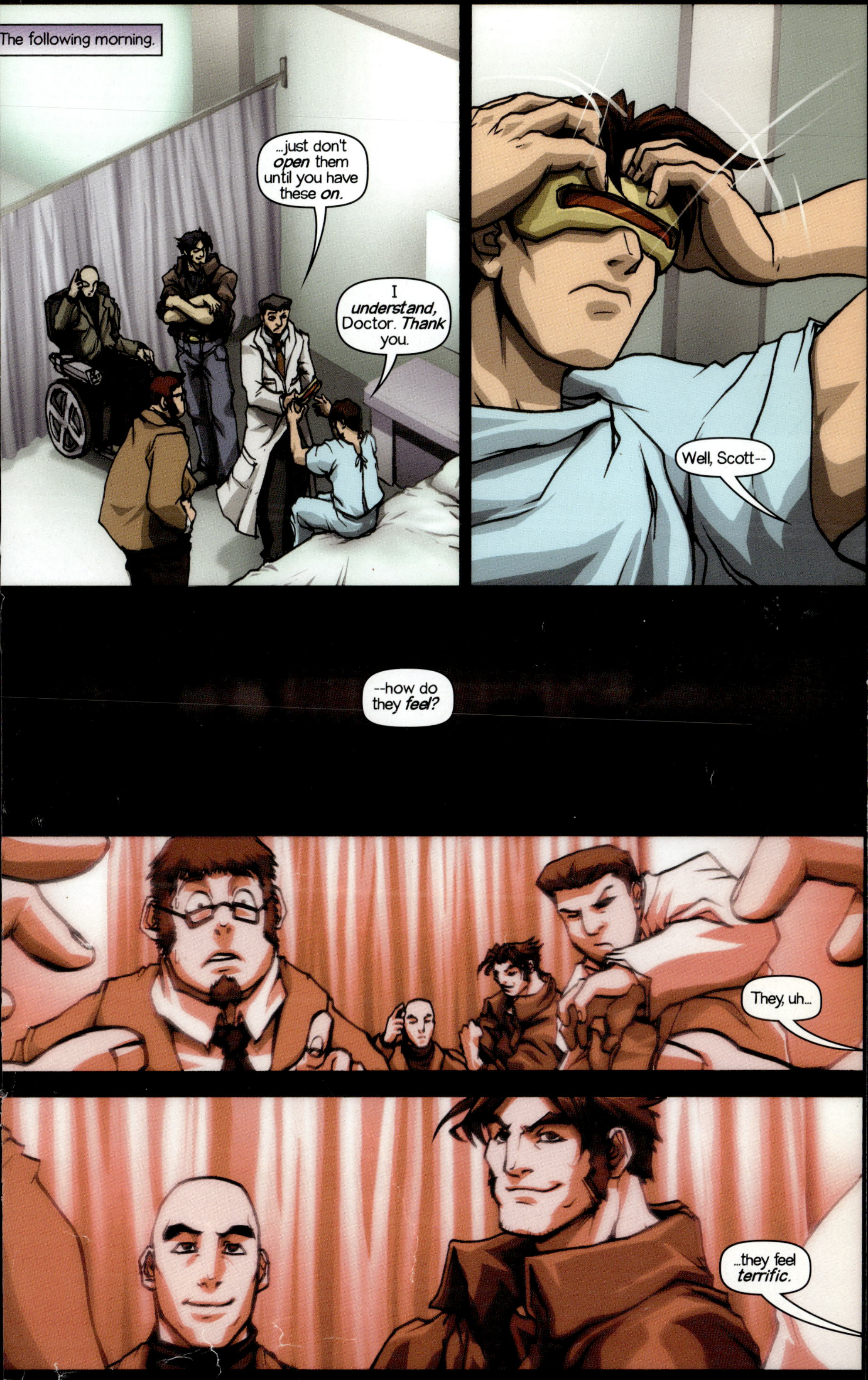

The following morning.
...just don't *open* them until you have these *on.*
I *understand,* Doctor. *Thank* you.
Well, Scott--
--how do they *feel?*
They, uh...
...they feel *terrific.*

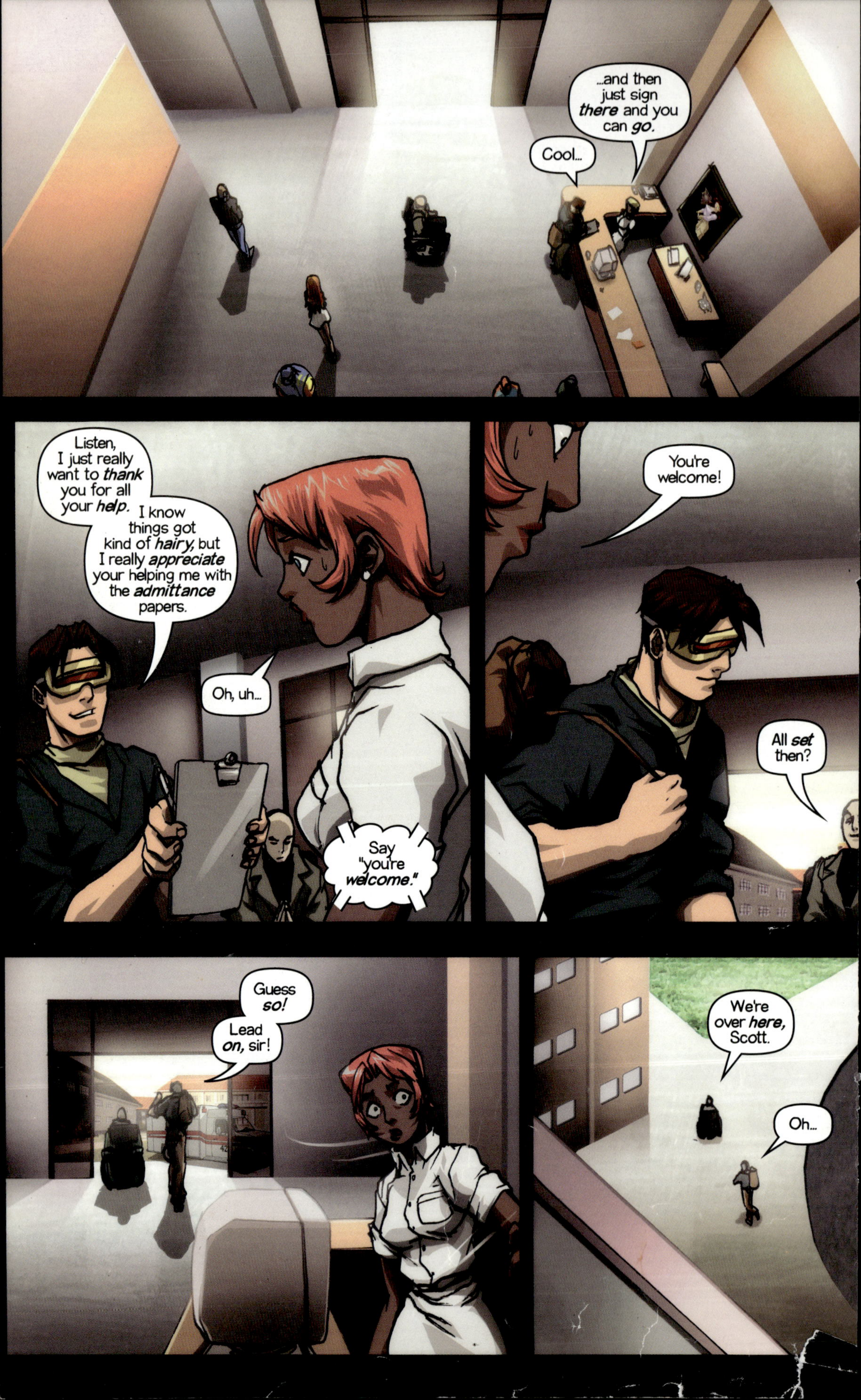
...and then just sign *there* and you can *go.*
Cool...
Listen, I just really want to *thank* you for all your *help.* I know things got kind of *hairy,* but I really *appreciate* your helping me with the *admittance* papers.
Oh, uh...
Say "you're *welcome."*
You're welcome!
All *set* then?
Guess *so!*
Lead *on,* sir!
We're over *here,* Scott.
Oh...

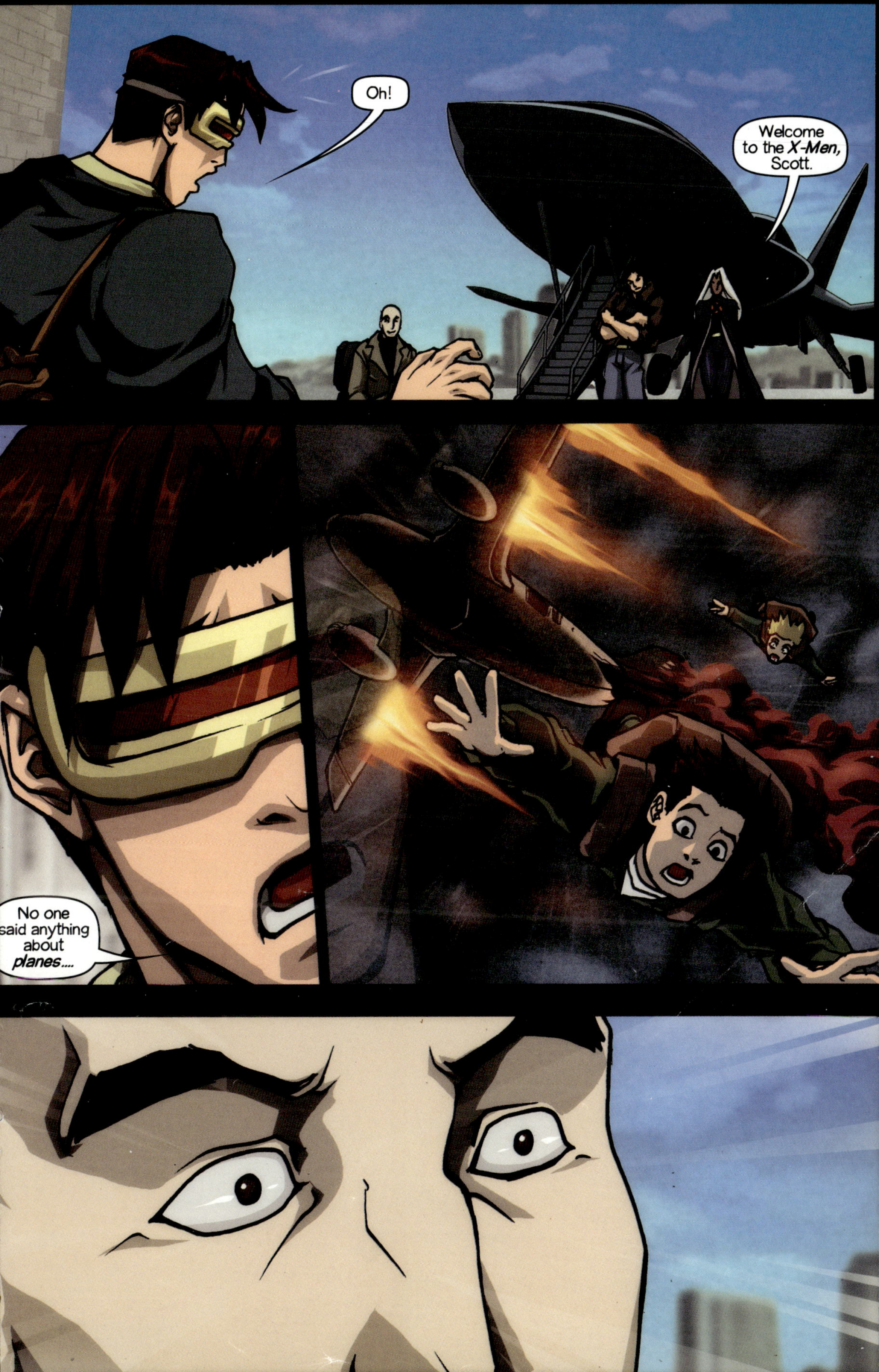
Oh!
Welcome to the *X-Men,* Scott.
No one said anything about *planes*....

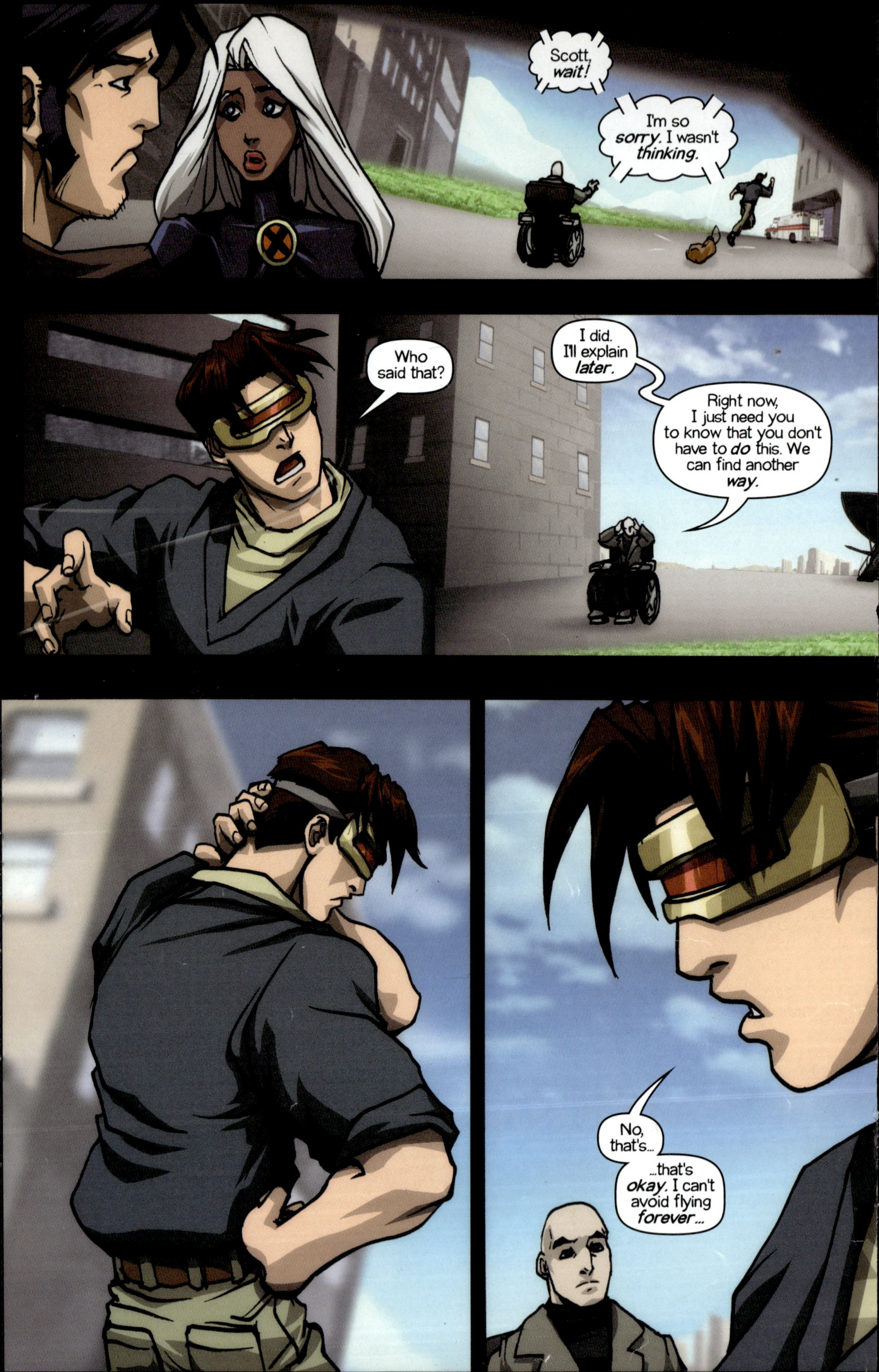

Scott, *wait!*
I'm so *sorry*. I wasn't *thinking*.
Who said that?
I did. I'll explain *later*.
Right now, I just need you to know that you don't have to *do* this. We can find another *way*.
No, that's...
...that's *okay*. I can't avoid flying *forever*...

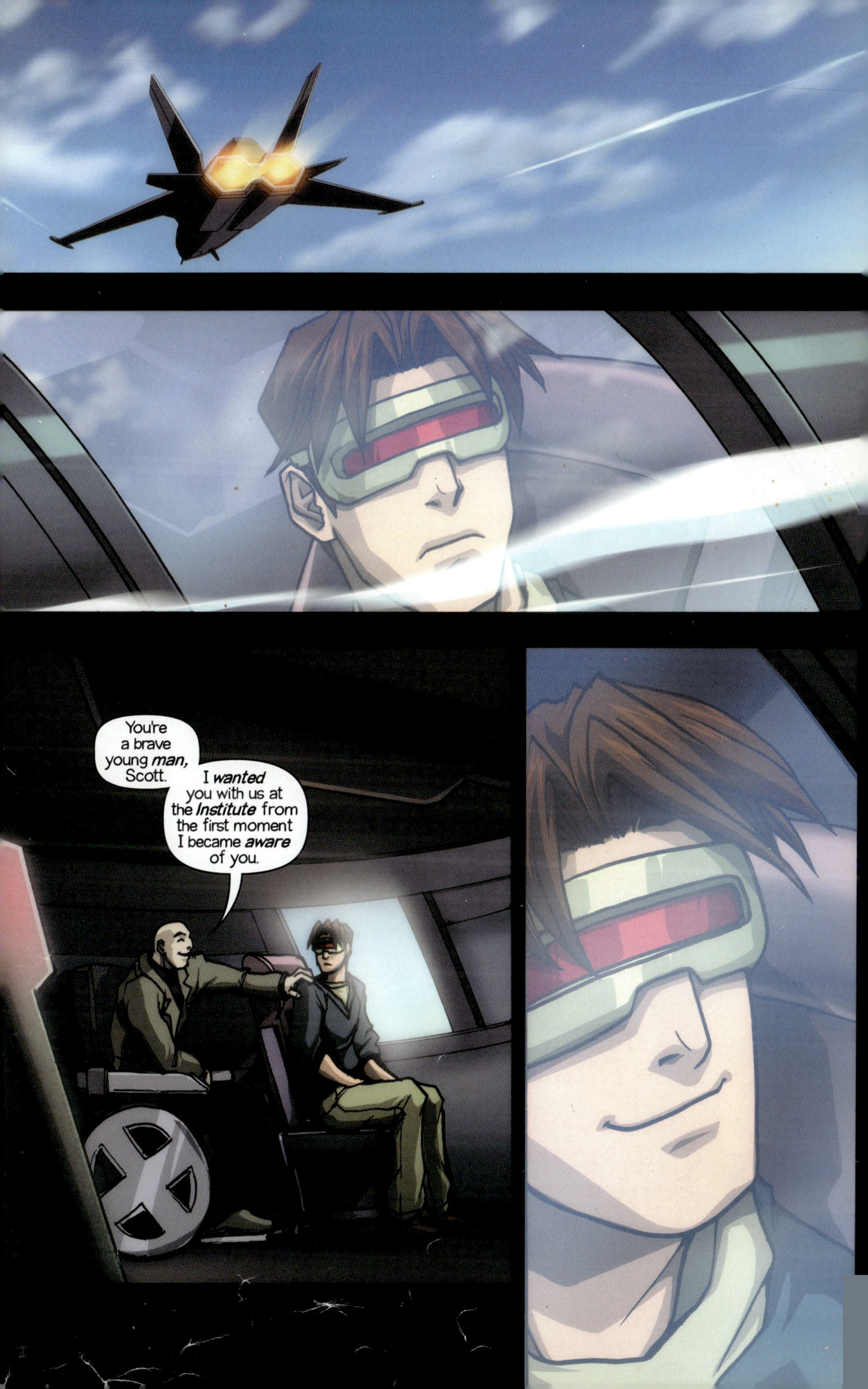
You're a brave young *man,* Scott.
I *wanted* you with us at the *Institute* from the first moment I became *aware* of you.

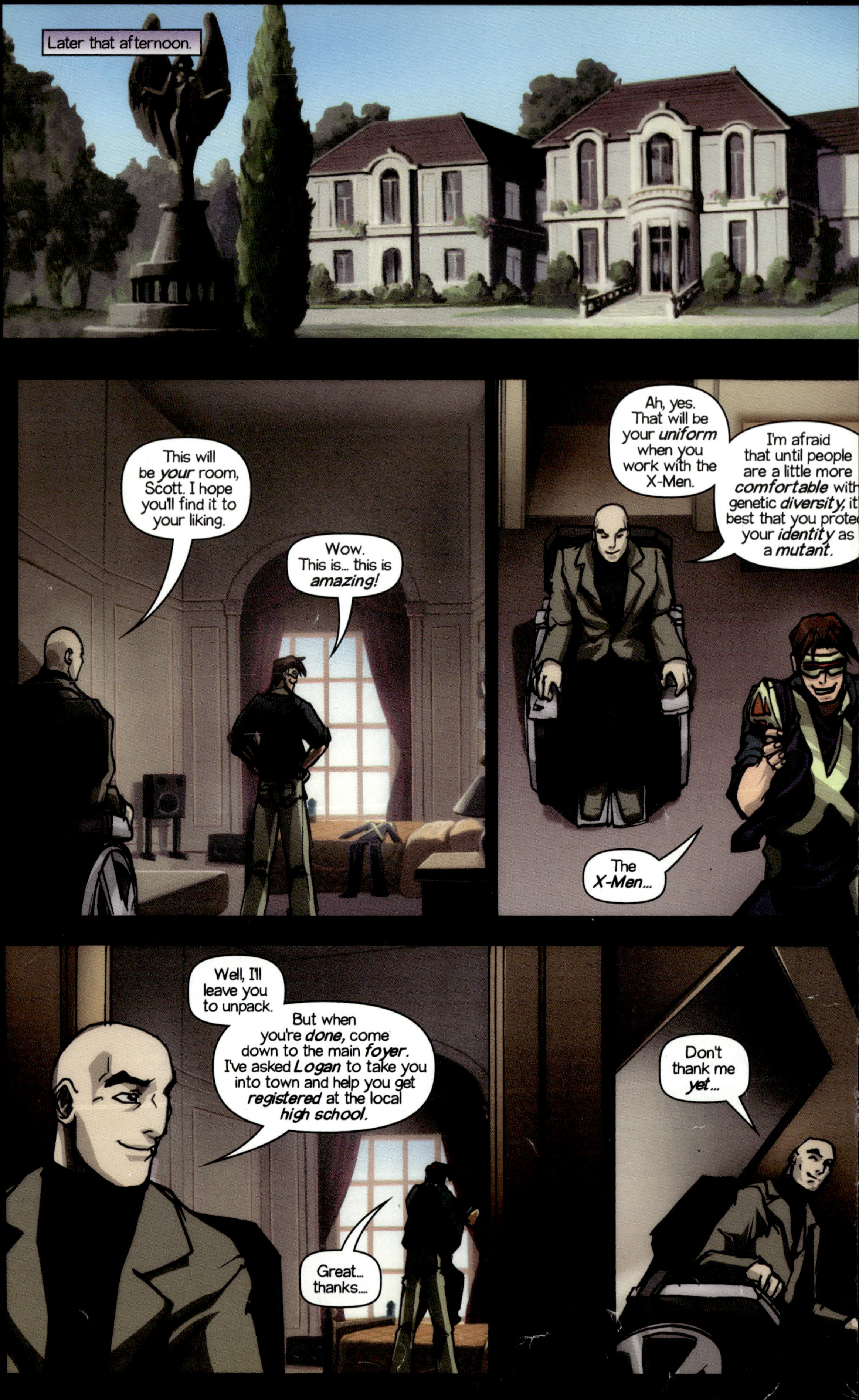

Later that afternoon.
This will be your room, Scott. I hope you'll find it to your liking.
Wow. This is... this is amazing!
Ah, yes. That will be your uniform when you work with the X-Men.
I'm afraid that until people are a little more comfortable wit genetic diversity, it best that you prote your identity as a mutant.
The X-Men...
Well, I'll leave you to unpack.
But when you're done, come down to the main foyer. I've asked Logan to take you into town and help you get registered at the local high school.
Great... thanks....
Don't thank me yet...

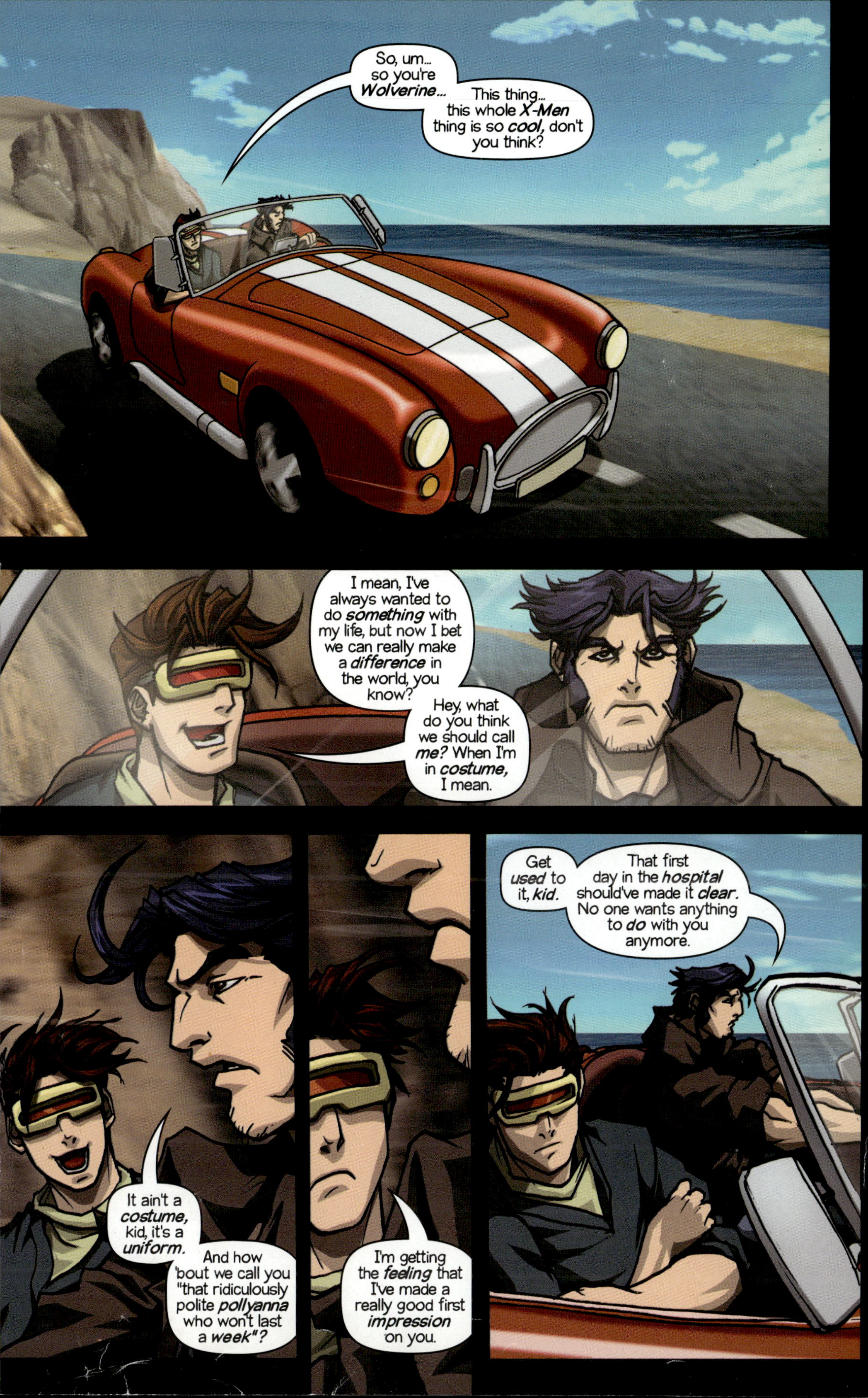
So, um... so you're *Wolverine*...
This thing... this whole *X-Men* thing is so *cool,* don't you think?
I mean, I've always wanted to do *something* with my life, but now I bet we can really make a *difference* in the world, you know?
Hey, what do you think we should call *me?* When I'm in *costume,* I mean.
It ain't a *costume,* kid, it's a *uniform.*
And how 'bout we call you "that ridiculously polite *pollyanna* who won't last a *week*"?
I'm getting the *feeling* that I've made a really good first *impression* on you.
Get *used* to it, *kid.*
That first day in the *hospital* should've made it *clear.* No one wants anything to *do* with you anymore.

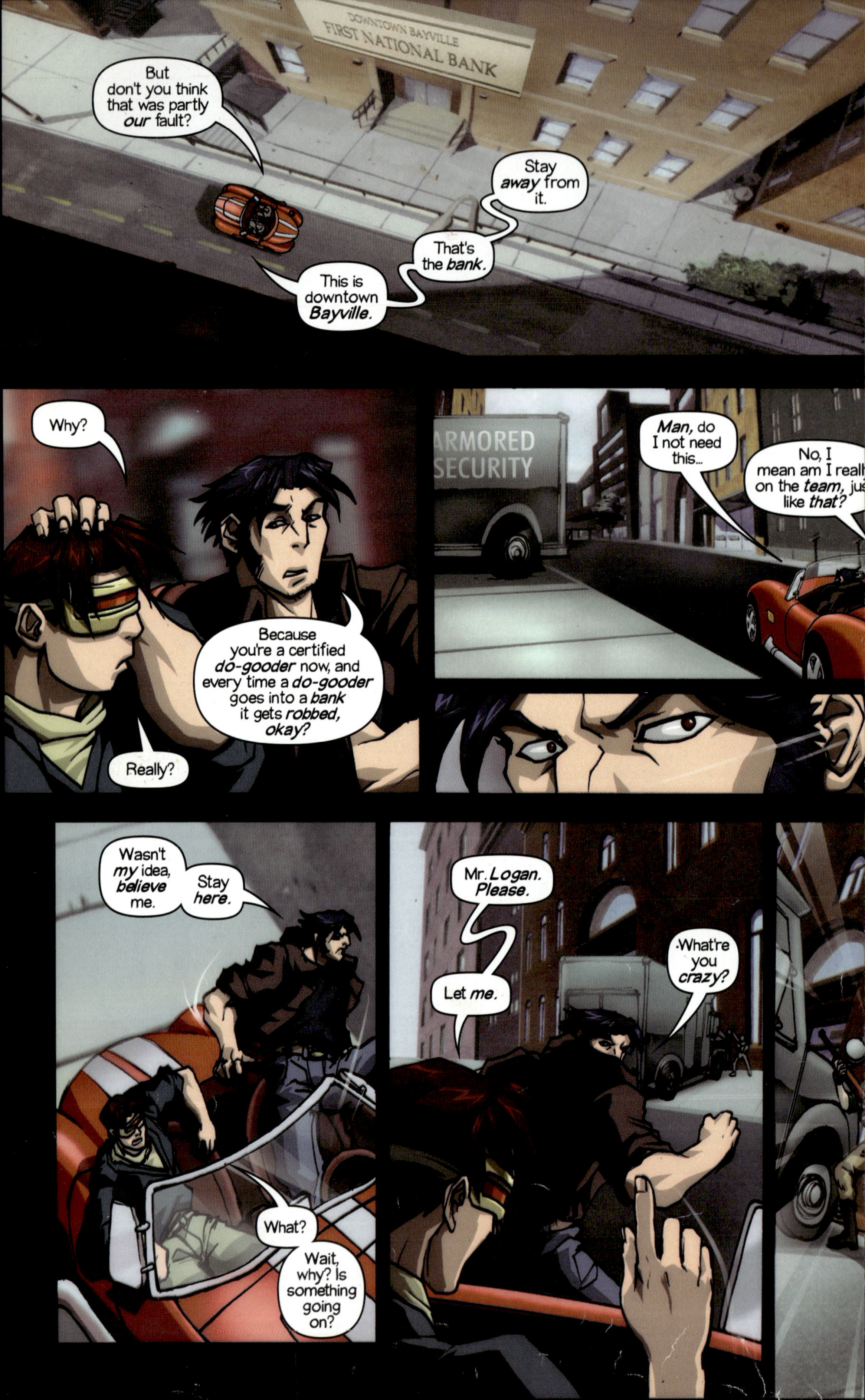
DOWNTOWN BAYVILLE
FIRST NATIONAL BANK
But don't you think that was partly our fault?
Stay away from it.
That's the bank.
This is downtown Bayville.
Why?
Because you're a certified do-gooder now, and every time a do-gooder goes into a bank it gets robbed, okay?
Really?
ARMORED SECURITY
Man, do I not need this...
No, I mean am I reall on the team, jus like that?
Wasn't my idea, believe me.
Stay here.
What?
Wait, why? Is something going on?
Mr. Logan. Please.
Let me.
What're you crazy?

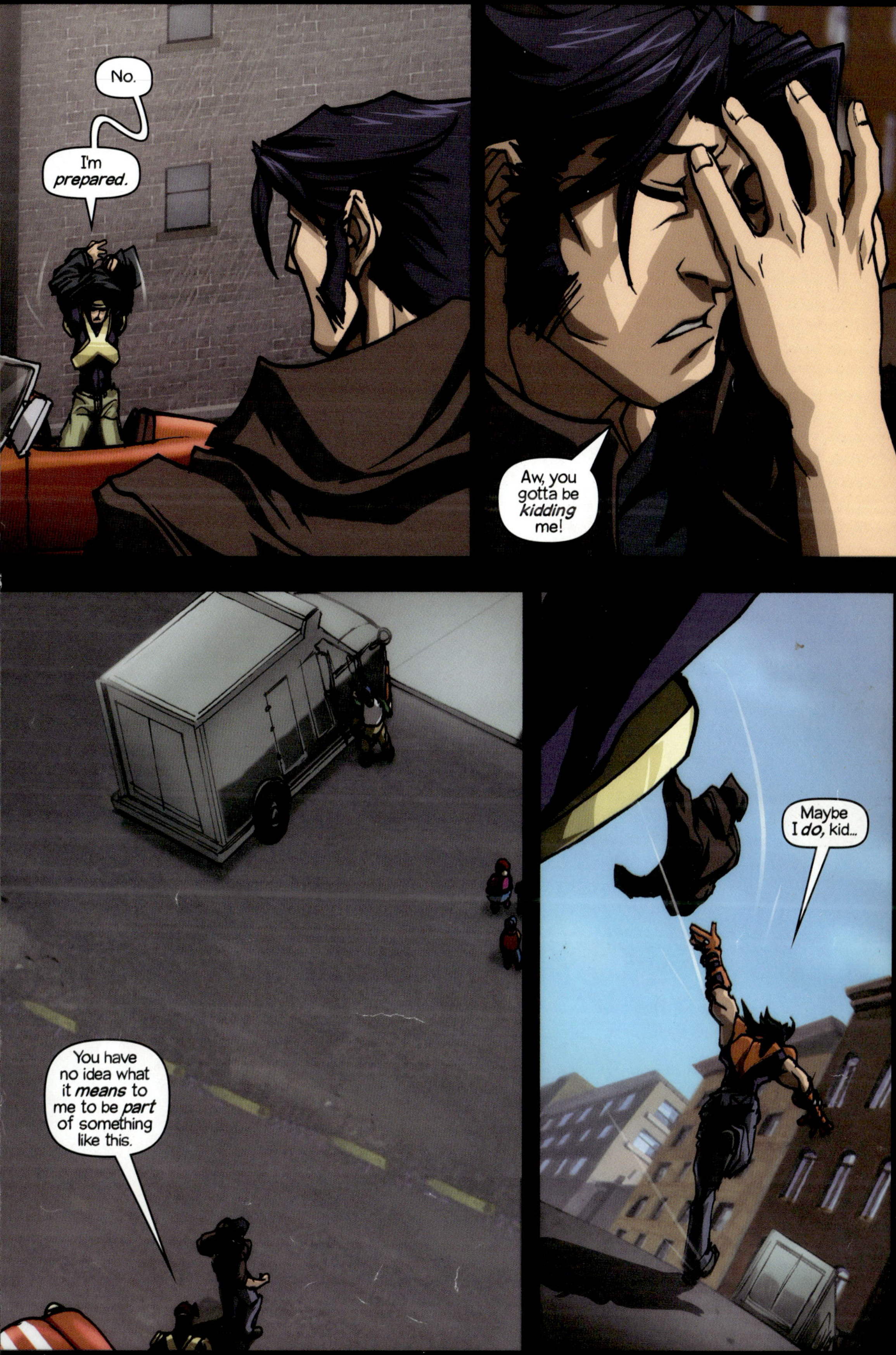
No.
I'm *prepared.*
Aw, you gotta be *kidding* me!
You have no idea what it *means* to me to be *part* of something like this.
Maybe I *do,* kid...

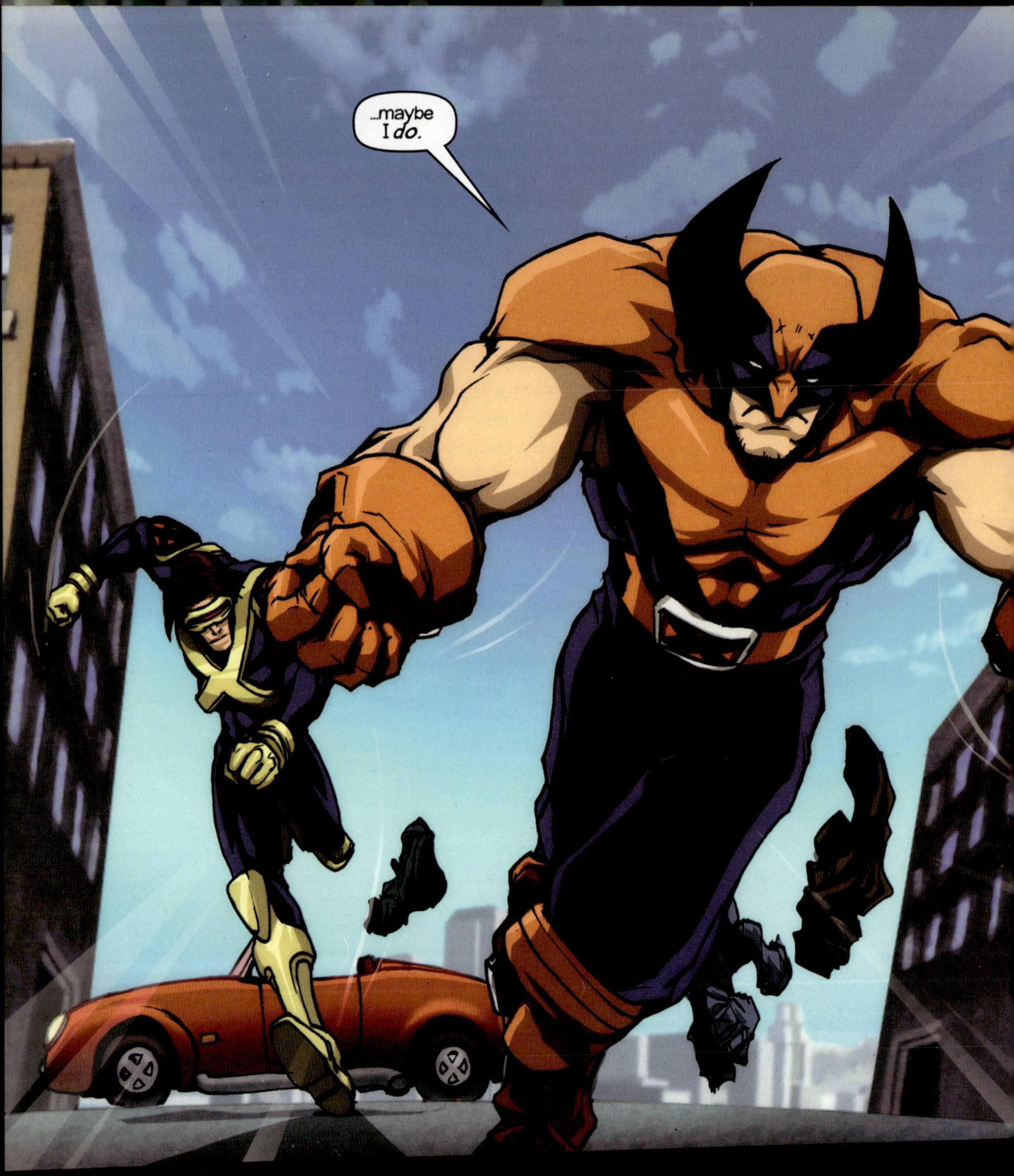
...maybe I *do*.

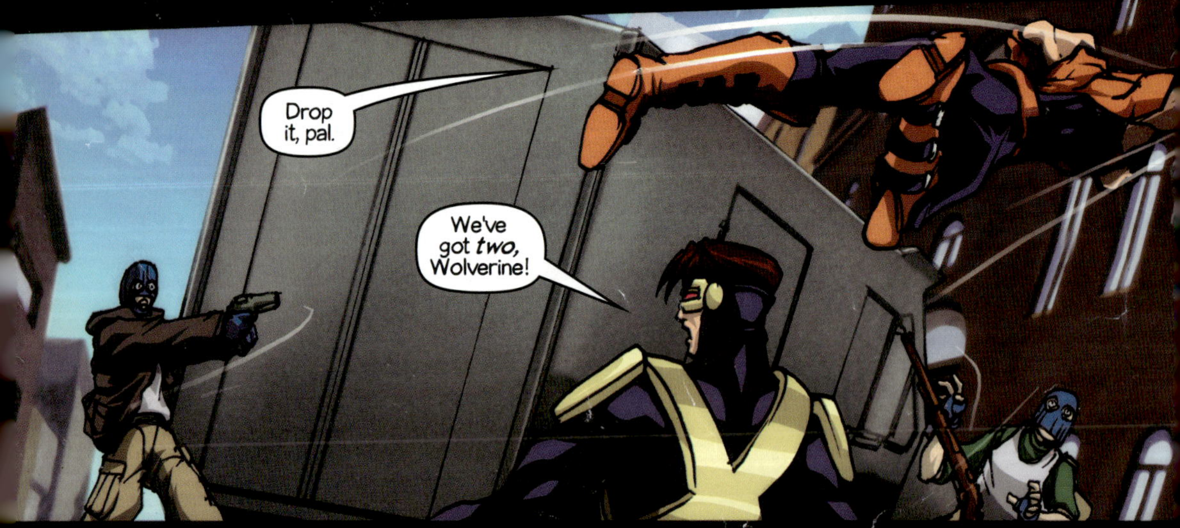
Drop it, pal.
We've got *two*, Wolverine!

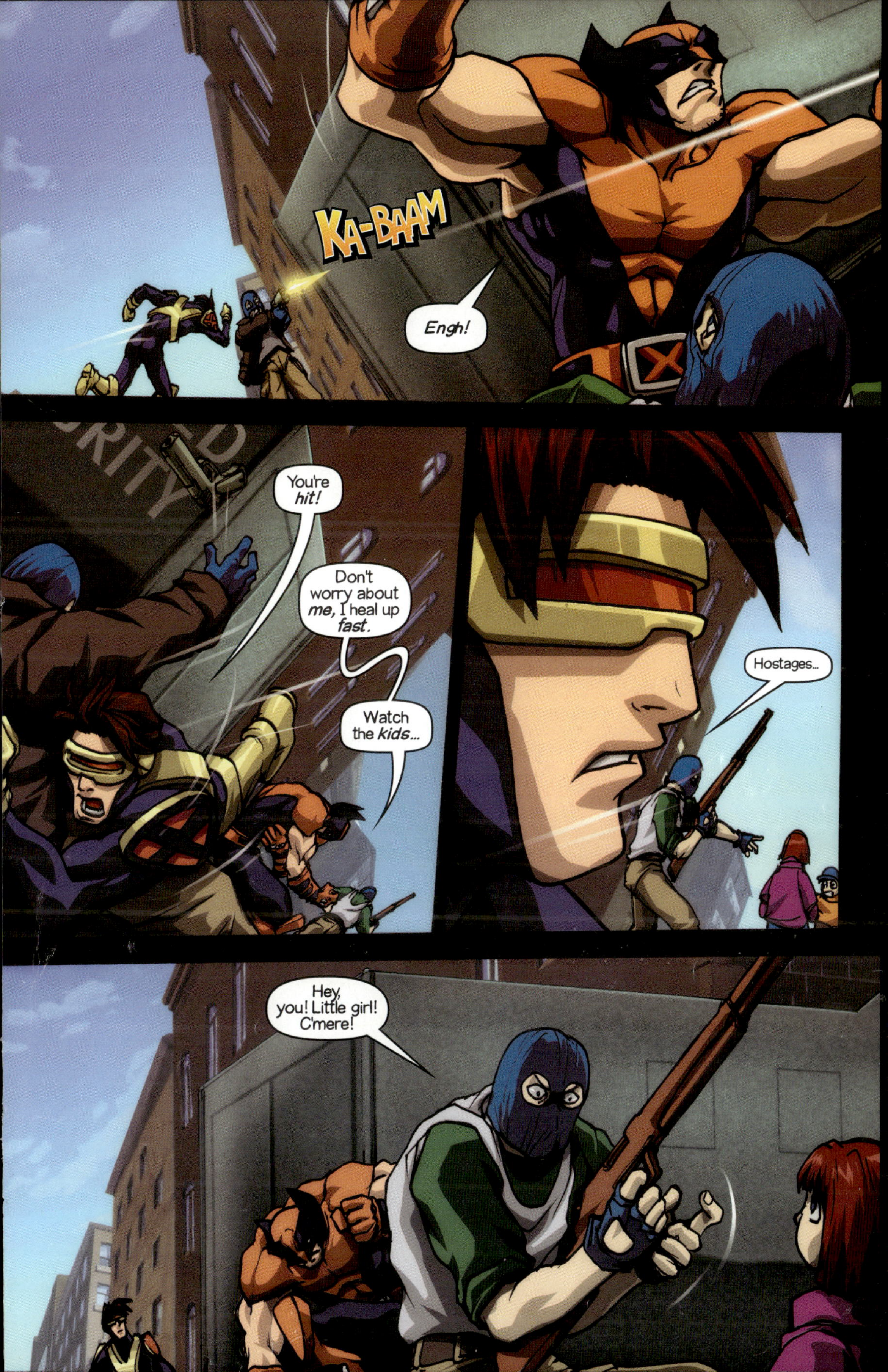
KA-BAAM
Engh!
You're hit!
Don't worry about me, I heal up fast.
Watch the kids...
Hostages...
Hey, you! Little girl! C'mere!

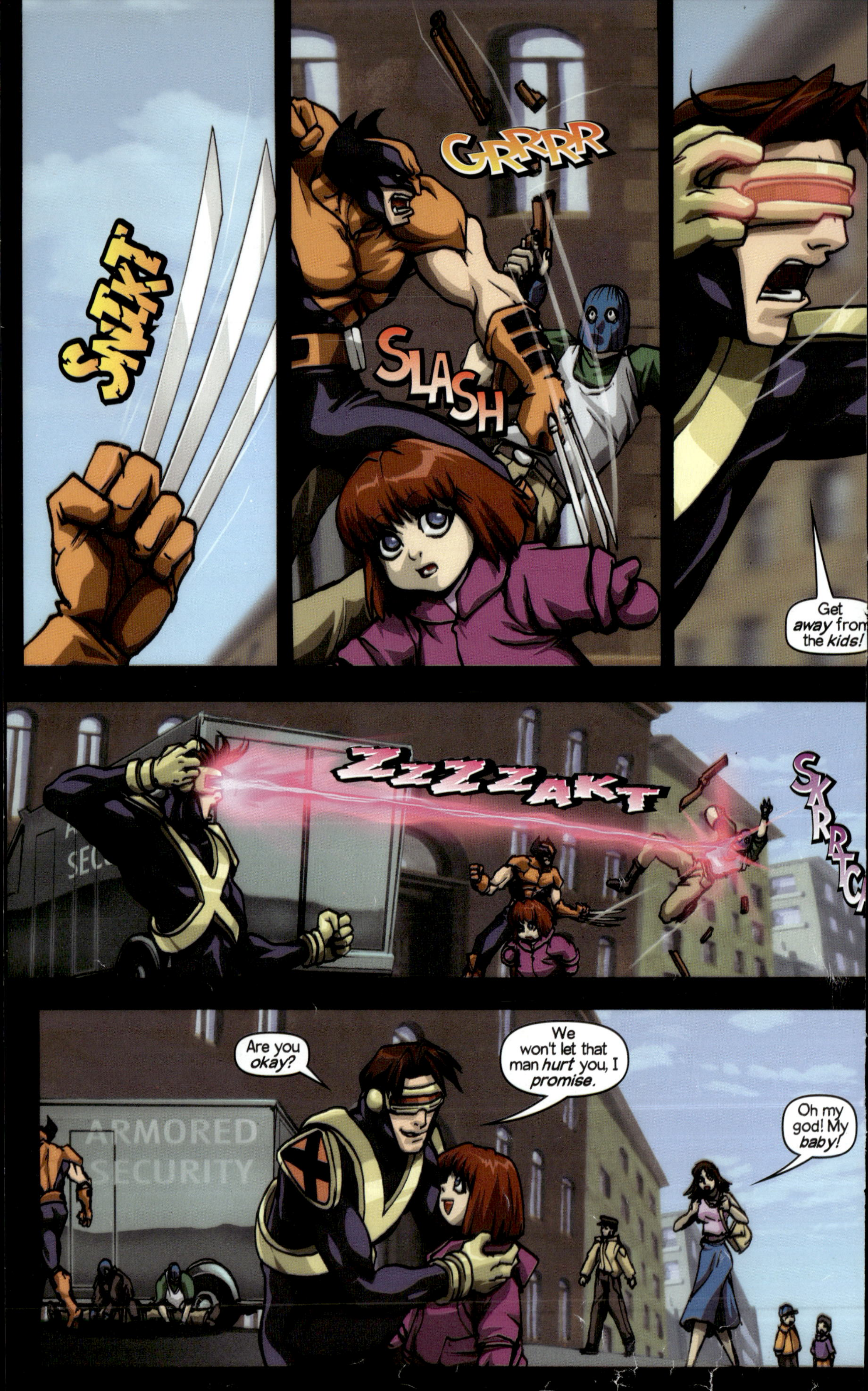
SNIKT
GRRRR
SLASH
Get *away* from the *kids!*
ZZZZAKT
SKRRTCH
Are you *okay?*
We won't let that man *hurt* you, I *promise.*
Oh my god! My *baby!*
ARMORED SECURITY

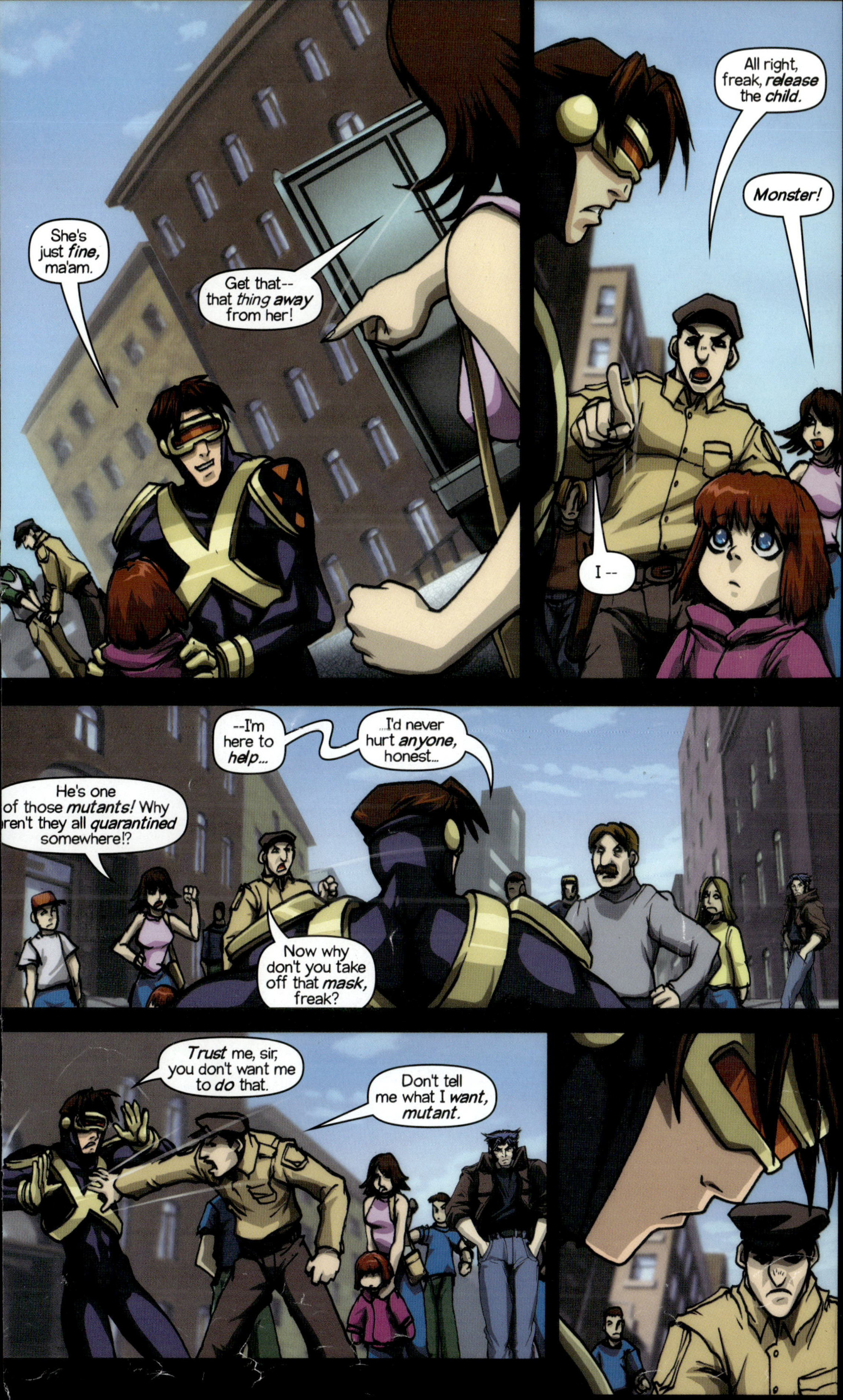
She's just *fine,* ma'am.
Get that-- that *thing away* from her!
All right, freak, *release* the *child.*
Monster!
I --
He's one of those *mutants!* Why ren't they all *quarantined* somewhere!?
--I'm here to *help...*
...I'd never hurt *anyone,* honest...
Now why don't you take off that *mask,* freak?
Trust me, sir, you don't want me to *do* that.
Don't tell me what I *want, mutant.*

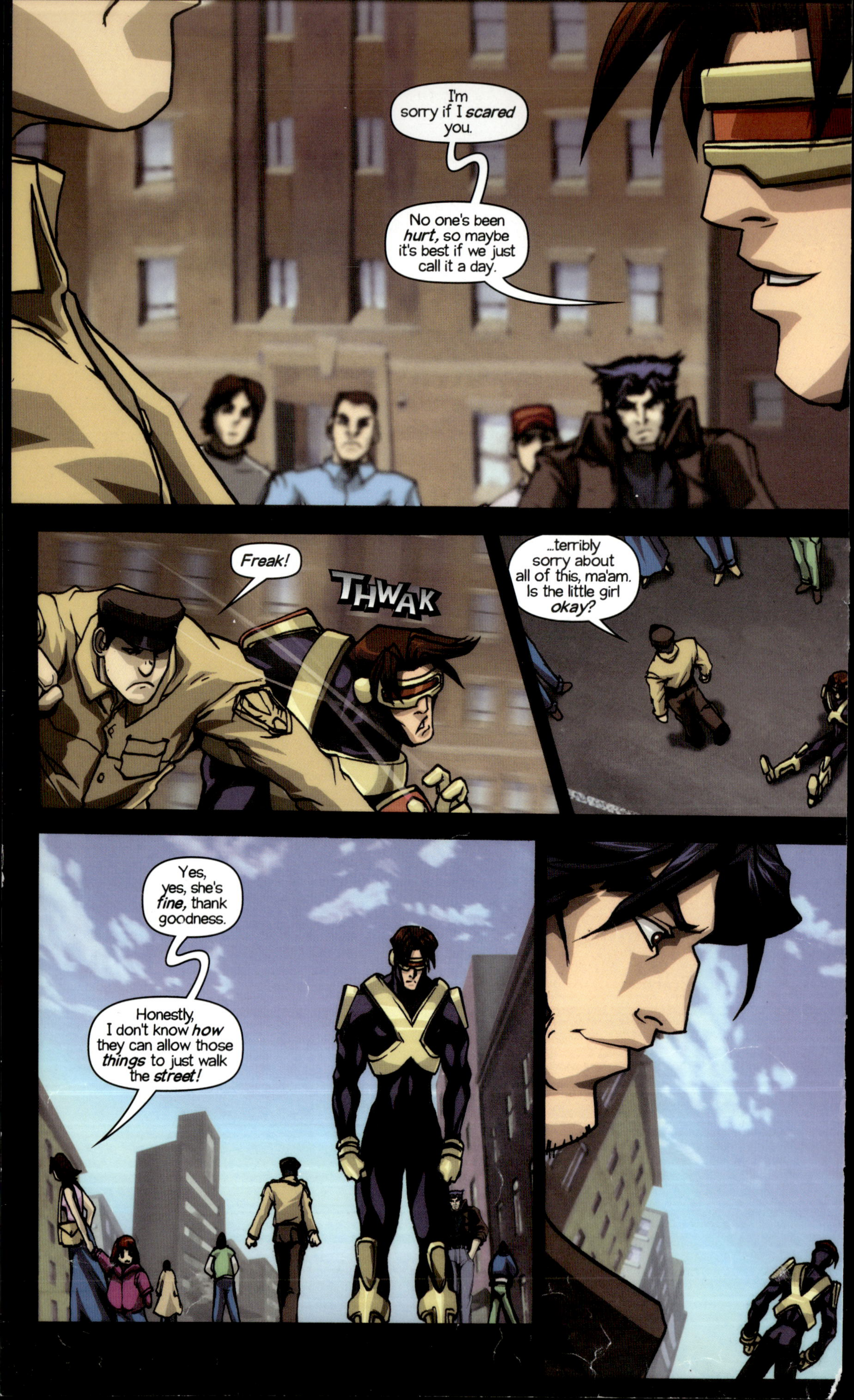
I'm sorry if I *scared* you.
No one's been *hurt,* so maybe it's best if we just call it a day.
Freak!
THWAK
...terribly sorry about all of this, ma'am. Is the little girl *okay?*
Yes, yes, she's *fine,* thank goodness.
Honestly, I don't know *how* they can allow those *things* to just walk the *street!*

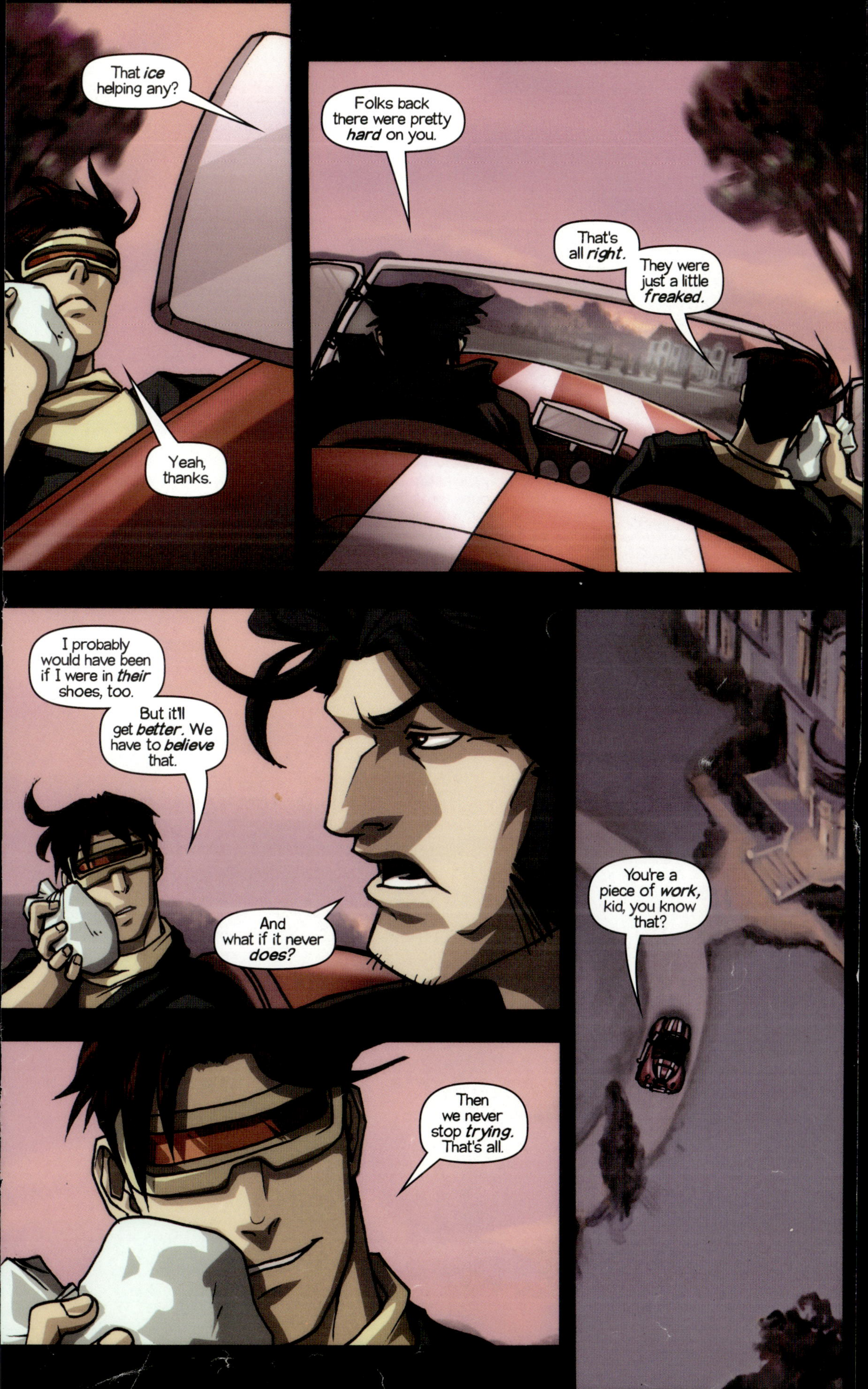
That *ice* helping any?
Yeah, thanks.
Folks back there were pretty *hard* on you.
That's all *right*.
They were just a little *freaked*.
I probably would have been if I were in *their* shoes, too.
But it'll get *better*. We have to *believe* that.
And what if it never *does?*
You're a piece of *work*, kid, you know that?
Then we never stop *trying*. That's all.

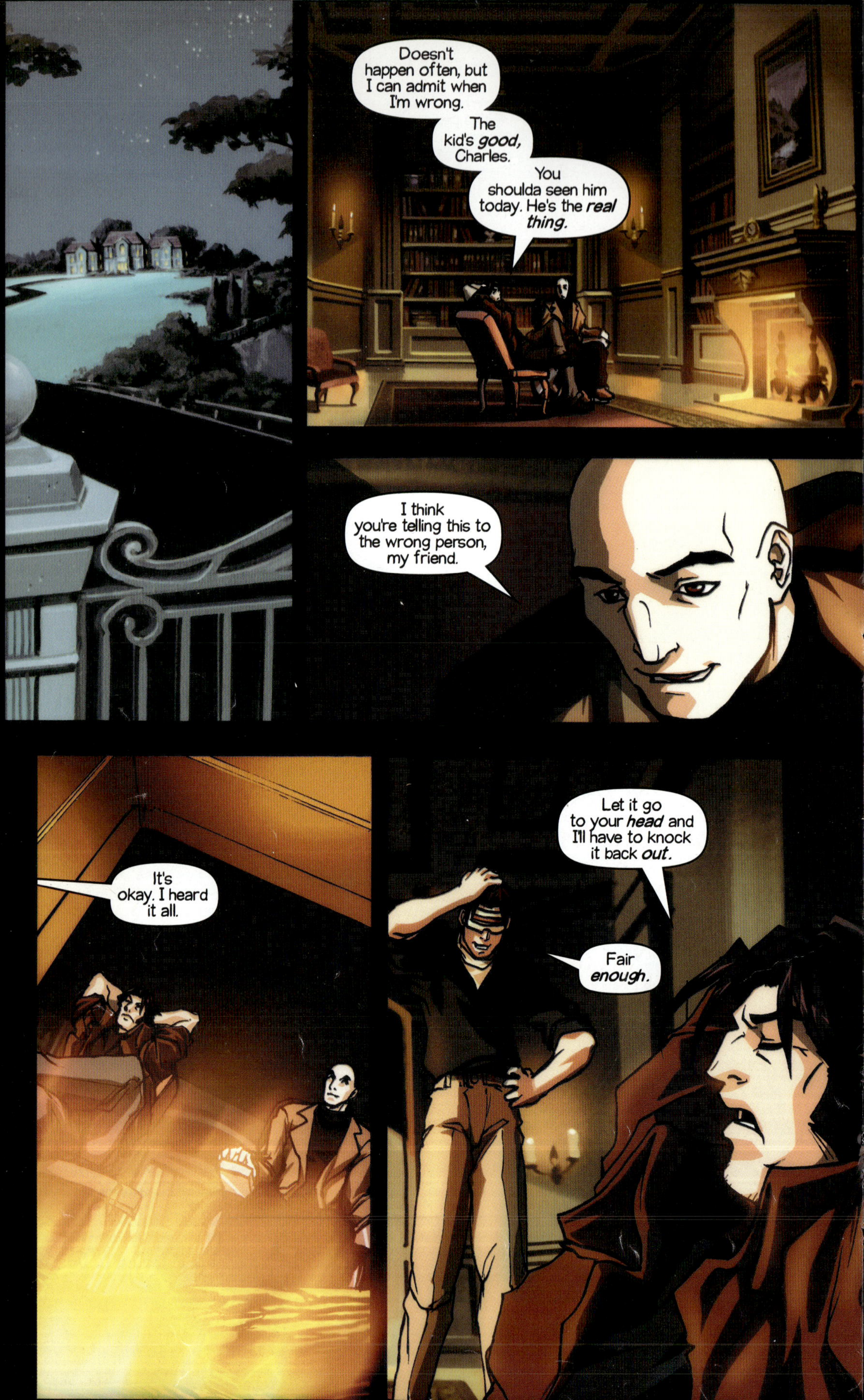
Doesn't happen often, but I can admit when I'm wrong.
The kid's *good,* Charles.
You shoulda seen him today. He's the *real thing.*
I think you're telling this to the wrong person, my friend.
It's okay. I heard it all.
Let it go to your *head* and I'll have to knock it back *out.*
Fair *enough.*

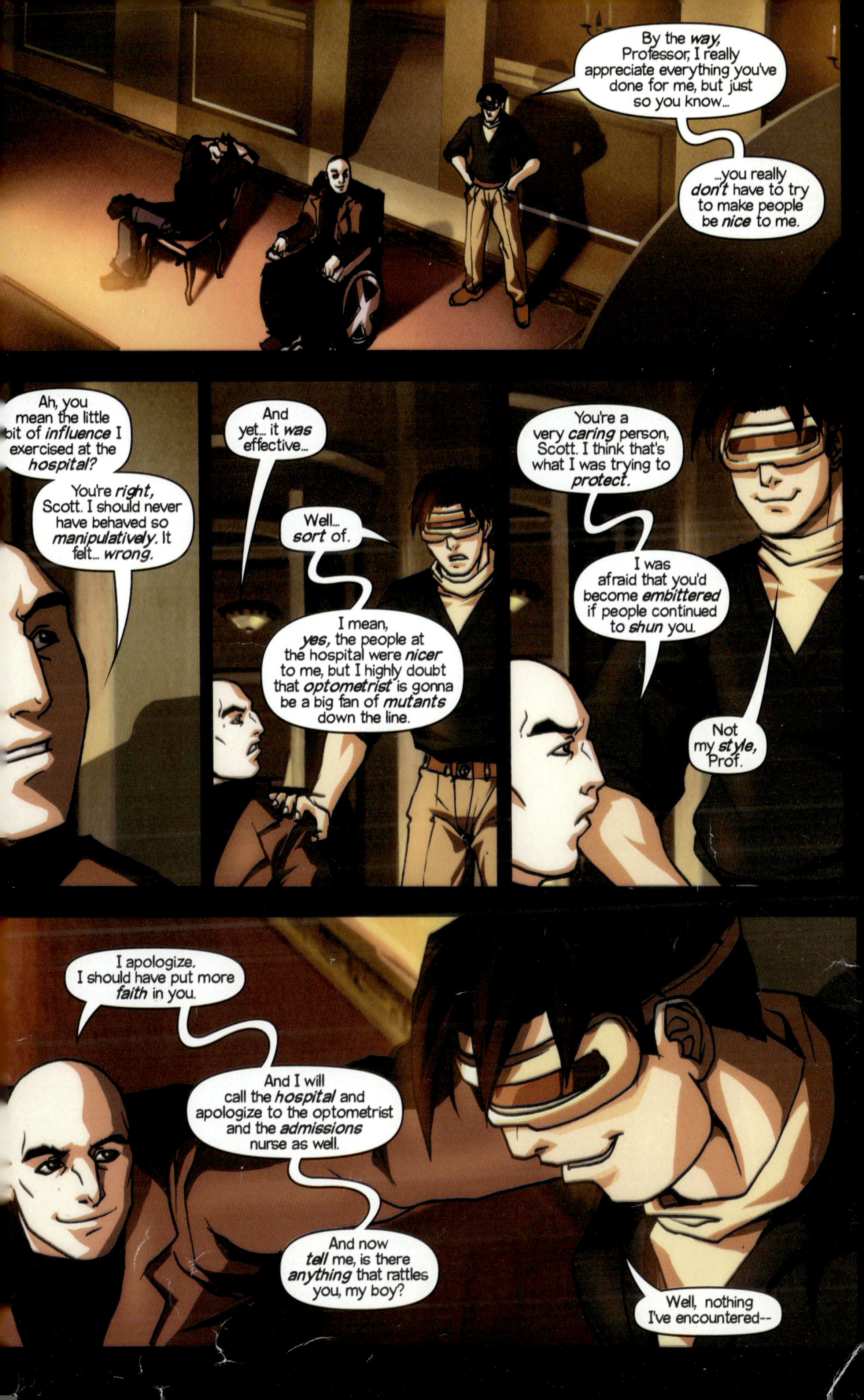
By the *way,* Professor, I really appreciate everything you've done for me, but just so you know...
...you really ***don't*** have to try to make people be ***nice*** to me.
Ah, you mean the little bit of ***influence*** I exercised at the ***hospital?***
You're ***right,*** Scott. I should never have behaved so ***manipulatively.*** It felt... ***wrong.***
And yet... it ***was*** effective...
Well... ***sort*** of.
I mean, ***yes,*** the people at the hospital were ***nicer*** to me, but I highly doubt that ***optometrist*** is gonna be a big fan of ***mutants*** down the line.
You're a very ***caring*** person, Scott. I think that's what I was trying to ***protect.***
I was afraid that you'd become ***embittered*** if people continued to ***shun*** you.
Not my ***style,*** Prof.
I apologize. I should have put more ***faith*** in you.
And I will call the ***hospital*** and apologize to the optometrist and the ***admissions*** nurse as well.
And now ***tell*** me, is there ***anything*** that rattles you, my boy?
Well, nothing I've encountered--

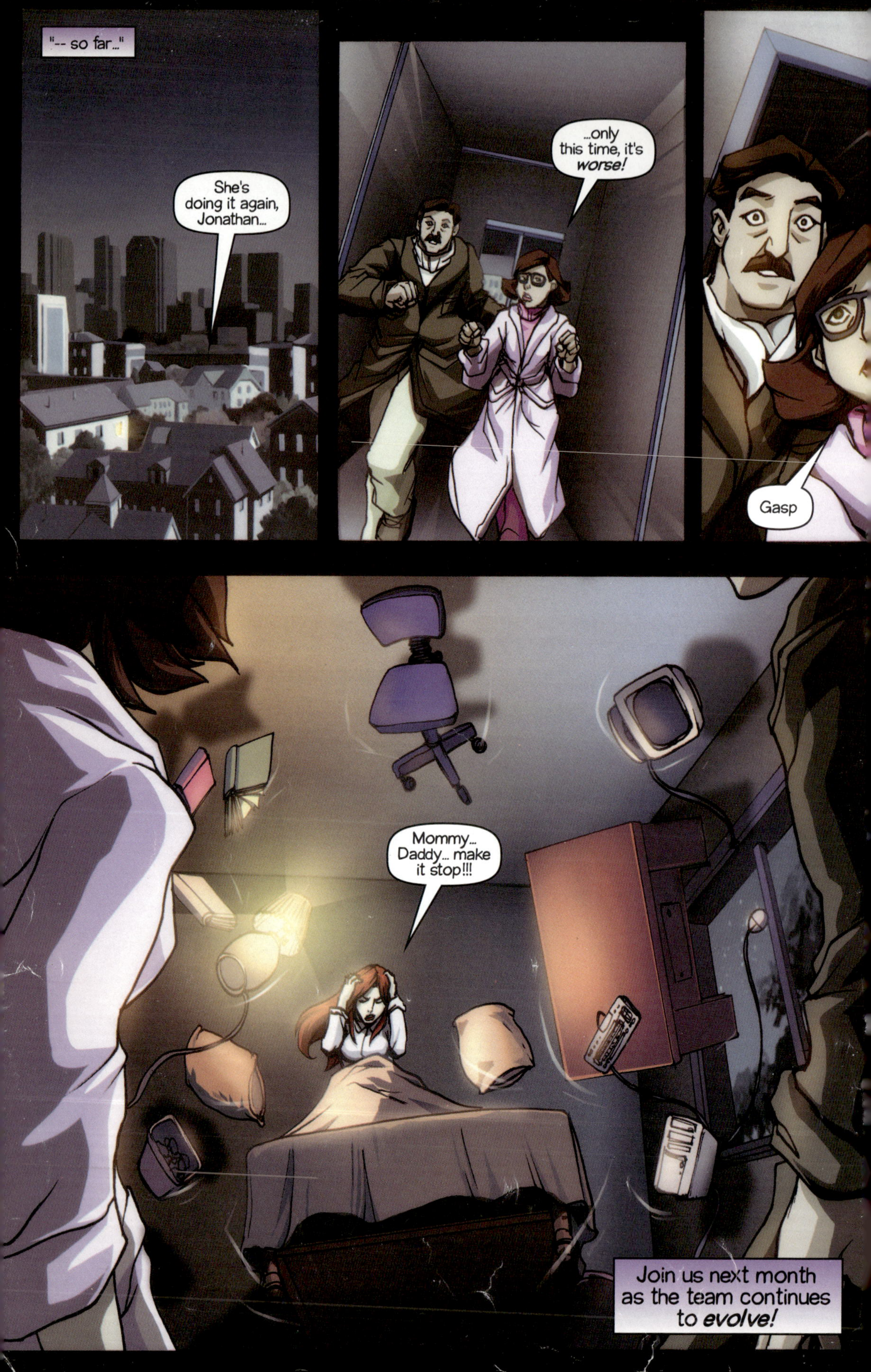
"-- so far..."
She's doing it again, Jonathan...
...only this time, it's *worse!*
Gasp
Mommy... Daddy... make it stop!!!
Join us next month as the team continues to *evolve!*

Edison Twp. Free Pub. Library
Clara Barton Branch
141 Hoover Ave.
Edison, NJ 08837

Edison Twp. Free Pub. Library
Clara Barton Branch
141 Hoover Ave.
Edison, NJ 08837